Amalia
Diary Three

Other books by Ann M. Martin

P.S. Longer Letter Later
(written with Paula Danziger)
Leo the Magnificat
Rachel Parker, Kindergarten Show-off
Eleven Kids, One Summer
Ma and Pa Dracula
Yours Turly, Shirley
Ten Kids, No Pets
Slam Book
Just a Summer Romance
Missing Since Monday
With You and Without You
Me and Katie (the Pest)
Stage Fright
Inside Out
Bummer Summer

THE KIDS IN MS. COLMAN'S CLASS series
BABY-SITTERS LITTLE SISTER series
THE BABY-SITTERS CLUB mysteries
THE BABY-SITTERS CLUB series
CALIFORNIA DIARIES series

California Diaries #14

Amalia
Diary Three

Ann M. Martin

SCHOLASTIC INC.
New York Toronto London Auckland Sydney
Mexico City New Delhi Hong Kong

Interior illustrations
by
Stieg Retlin

No part of this publication may be reproduced in whole or in part, or stored in a retrieval system, or transmitted in any form or by any means, electronic, mechanical, photocopying, recording, or otherwise, without written permission of the publisher. For information regarding permission, write to Scholastic Inc., Attention: Permissions Department, 555 Broadway, New York, NY 10012.

ISBN 0-439-09548-4

12 11 10 9 8 7 6 5 4 3 2 1   0/0 1 2 3 4 5/0

Printed in the U.S.A.   40
First Scholastic printing, April 2000

The author gratefully acknowledges
Peter Lerangis
for his help in
preparing this manuscript.

Amalia
Diary Three

Tuesday, 5/25

I knew it, Nbook.

Did I predict it or what?

When Maggie tells me about meeting Tyler Kendall and informs me that she HATES him, do I believe her?

No way.

Fact: For Maggie, "I hate Tyler" means "I hate Hollywood" means "I hate the fact that Dad is Hayden Blume the famous producer who works seven days a week and never comes home until midnight."

Fact: Tyler's OK. Fact: He likes

her. Fact: He doesn't give up so
easily.

So now she's singing a different
tune.

THE TRUTH

It's good to see Maggie so happy.
And not just because of Tyler.

She's kicking the anorexia. I can
tell.

I predicted that too. And I was
right.

Wednesday, 5/26

As for me? Thanks for asking,
Nbook.

Haven't felt better.

It's a little scary.

EXTRA☆☆PALO CITY POST☆☆EXTRA
AMALIA VARGAS
is
HAPPY
Miracle in Southern California:
Exclusive—How Her Life Has Changed
End-of-Year Wrap-up

III Amigas

Maggie
(see yesterday)
Sunny and Dawn

Rest in peace, Mrs. W, your daughter is going to be all right. Her friends will see to that.

Sunny is an inspiration, Nbook.
Her mom's death hit her hard. But she's pulling herself together. Somehow.
I admire her.
I admire all my friends.
How did I get so lucky?
Maggie's here. Time to go.

Thursday, 5/27
Lunch

Big news. Double date tomorrow night. Same as last time. Me and

Brendan, Maggie and Tyler (I guess
"double date" isn't the right term.
Tyler and Maggie are the Real
Thing, boyfriend-girlfriend. Way ahead
of us. Call it a date and a half.
Whatever.)

I just hope people don't drool all
over him again. (Tyler, that is. Not
Brendan. He's not the movie star —
although he could be. But that's
another conversation.)

Sorry about the chocolate shake
stain. (Guess I shouldn't open you
during lunch.)

Don't you love ~~parenthesises~~
parentheses? (Yes.)

4:47

Stupid, stupid, stupid.

Why do I bother telling Isabel
about my personal life?

Why do I let her see me
happy?

Here's what happens.

AmaliaVargasdon'tyourealizeit'salmostJuneandthat meansEXAMS—I'malreadystudyingPLUS I'm done with homework—that's called RESPONSIBILITY and all you're doing is DREAMING and DROOLING and OBSESSING about your friends like everything's going to take care of itself—and what about summer plans and yada yada yada...

Must be tough to be perfect.

7:35

Maggie comes over just before dinner tonight. Last-minute thing. Says Zeke is at a friend's, her dad's at work (as usual), and her mom's "out."

She's not feeling too great. Says she feels tense all the time.

As we're talking, I hear Simon Big

Tooth Lover Boy's old car pull up. Then I hear him downstairs in the kitchen with Isabel.

And she's explaining her homework to him.

Yes, _that_ homework. Which she does _early_ because she's so _responsible_. . . .

What a phony.

Flash: Brendan has a new shirt and shoes. (Yes, Nbook, the Boy Who Hates to shop. The boy who claims his faded amber Grateful Dead T-shirt is actually white. Translation: It was white when his dad wore it in 1983.)

Well, the clothes are a pleasant surprise. So is the haircut.

When I notice the cuts on his cheek, though, I become suspicious. I ask who scratched him, and he says, "I shaved."

"Shaved what?" I ask.

He does not see the humor.

Guess I have to look at this from his point of view. I mean, if I were a guy soon to be on a double date and the other guy on that date was Tyler Kendall, wouldn't I be nervous about my appearance?

I tell him not to worry. He doesn't have to be a hunk. I like him just the way he is.

He says, "I'm not a hunk?"

I pretend to think about it.

He still doesn't see the humor.

Poor soul.

Late late late late so-o-o-o late
I'm back. I'm alive. I'm awake.

How was my night?

I might as well have been in outer space.

That's what it felt like. A trip to Pluto.

NOTE TO SELF: Learn from

experience. Bring rugged clothes to next experience with Maggie and Tyler. Maybe a sword and shield.

Here's us walking toward the restaurant:

Here's us when we get into the restaurant:

The meal? The view?

No meal. No view. This time Tyler doesn't just stand there, smiling and chatting, while we suffer. Instead, he politely signs a few autographs, excuses himself, and heads back out, pulling us with him. (Got to give him credit. He must have listened to Maggie's advice after last time.)

Anyway, we leave the restaurant and sneak into a 9:00 showing at the Rubicon Theater. The cuisine is popcorn and Snickers.

No one else is in the theater. The air-conditioning is way too high.

And the movie is in Russian, so you have to read subtitles.

Maggie insists it is a great classic.

Me, I don't understand a thing.

Brendan hates it. He says I owe him one.

I'll make it up to him. Next time, we go to the cineplex to see a good, stupid American comedy.

I'm dreaming. Brendan and I are still at the Rubicon, only somehow we've stepped into the movie. We're stranded on the frozen tundra in our shorts and sandals. We're clutching each other tight, trying to keep warm — and we can see the audience staring, so we scream for help, but the words come out in Russian and everyone is laughing at us. . . .

And I hear:

I jump out of bed, thinking the tundra has been bombed

The reality: Isabel is clomping through my room, looking for something.

"What's up?" I say.

"Good morning to you too," she snaps. (Like, how dare I be rude to <u>her</u>?) Then her voice drops to a whisper: "Where's that rental car information?"

"What rental car —?"

"Ssssssshh, Mami and Papi will hear you. You know, the car for Hector and Cristina. Did you reserve one?"

"How could I do that? I'm thirteen —"

"With Hector and Cristina's credit card number, like I told you to —"

"You never —"

"Oh. I know, you're busy dating and hanging out with stars and preparing to flunk your finals. Guess they'll just have to <u>walk</u> the fifty-seven miles from the airport."

She leaves the room without even closing my door. I nearly throw my alarm clock at her.

Nbook, she <u>never</u> asked me to do this. (At least I don't think she did.) Besides, why can't Hector and Cristina rent the car themselves?

<u>And what's that crack about flunking my finals?</u> I know the material (mostly).

(Well, some, anyway.)
(I can study for the rest.)
(I better.)

11:23

I just looked at the math.
Remind me never, ever, ever to
open up a math book on a Saturday.
<u>What language is this stuff?</u>

Maggie calls. She apologizes about last night.

She hated the movie too. She was pretending to like it because she figured Tyler did. Turns out he slept through most of it.

I'm barely hearing her. I'm freaking about the finals. Especially math.

Finally I admit this to her.

She ignores me. Says she's spending the day with Tyler on the set. They're shooting extra footage for his latest movie — which was supposed to be finished, but they need some match prints (whatever they are). Anyway, they're going to have lunch at the food trailer.

"I'm going to flunk math," I persist.

She replies, "We'll swing by and pick you up."

"We'll?"

"Tyler and me. In the limo. Bring your math. I can help. We'll have plenty of time. You and I will just be

sitting around and eating while they
shoot."

Now we're talking.

I feel relieved.

And then I think — is this Maggie
talking about (a) actually going on a
movie set willingly and (b) eating?

I was right, Nbook. She's turning
the corner.

Progress, progress, progress.

I just hope she holds on. . . .

6:02 P.M.

Honestly, I think he reads my mind.

Just as Maggie's limo pulls up this
afternoon, Brendan calls. When he finds
out where I'm going, he practically
begs to come along.

I make him promise not to get in
the way of my remedial math. He
says he'll help Maggie help me.

So Maggie, Tyler, and I swing by
his house to pick him up. Here's what
we see:

　　His whole family's lined up outside
the house, along with neighbors and
their pets. To see the Star, of course.
Brendan is so embarrassed. He
apologizes like crazy.
　　Tyler's cool. He just waves back.
"You get used to it," he says.
　　We have a laugh about last night.
Then the boys start yakking away
about baseball and cars and stuff.
(This is how guys get to know each
other, Nbook. It's not who you are or
how you feel, but how many statistics
you know.) Anyway, just as I'm about

to fall asleep from boredom, Tyler
asks Brendan what he's doing for the
summer.

And Brendan says he's going to
camp.

For seven weeks.

In western Massachusetts.

Yes, you heard me right.

I believe it's somewhere around
<u>here</u>.

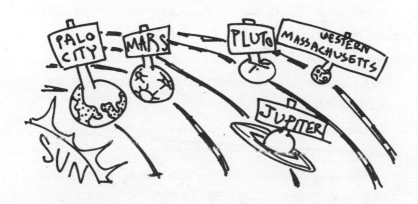

Yeah, OK, I knew he was going to
camp. I just didn't know where. I
guess we never discussed that.

What kid goes to summer camp clear across the continent?

Someone who used to live back East, that's who. (Nbook, why do people say "back East" but "out West"? I find it offensive. I don't know why, I just do.)

Brendan talks about how his parents used to drive him five hours from New Jersey to camp every summer, and now he can't imagine not going, because he's a CIT, yada yada yada. And I have no idea what a CIT is ("Coastally Insane Traveler"?), plus he doesn't seem the least bit . . . I don't know . . . thoughtful or doubtful or

SAD.

GUILTY.

BROKEN UP.

DEVASTATED NOT TO SEE ME FOR ALMOST TWO WHOLE MONTHS WHILE I SIT AROUND HERE WITH NOTHING TO DO.

There.

I got it out of my system.

It's really not that big a deal.

It's a free country. He can do whatever he wants.

Today, around noon, Maggie calls me and asks if I'm OK. She says I looked "upset" yesterday. (Am I the <u>worst</u> actor, Nbook? Am I <u>so</u> obvious?)

"I'm not upset," I lie.

"Don't worry, maybe you can visit him."

"In <u>western Massachusetts</u>? Do planes actually fly that far?"

She laughs and tells me she'll be right over. She says I need company.

Actually, I don't. I feel like being alone. (Obviously I don't tell her that.)

There's a pause. I can hear yelling in the background.

Maggie's voice drops to a whisper. "Um, I'll . . . be right over," she says again.

"Why? What hap —?"
Click.
About half an hour later, Maggie's limo is pulling up. When she steps out, she's carrying a duffel bag, and she's practically in tears. "What happened?" I ask.

"I. Can't. Live. With. Them."

I calm her down and invite her inside. As we sit on the living room sofa, she tells me the news: Her mom's drinking has gotten out of control. Mr. Blume wants her to go to the Betty Ford Clinic — but when he suggested it, she went ballistic.

Maggie asks if she can stay the night.

Of course I say yes.

All my little problems fly away, Nbook. I feel so bad for her.

I run out back. Mami and Papi are reading on the deck. When I tell them what happened, they agree to let Maggie stay. Mami suggests we borrow her bike and take a ride. Maybe that'll calm Maggie down.

Soon Maggie and I are heading to Las Palmas County Park. We sit on a bench and watch a pickup soccer game. A couple of families have spread out blankets and are eating a late lunch.

"You know the worst part?" she says. "Zeke. He's got this shell around him. He's, like, eleven going on thirty. Today he tells Mom to grow up. Right to her face. Dad starts screaming at him. Then Mom starts screaming at both of them. Then Dad screams at Mom. . . ."

"I thought she was getting better."

Maggie shrugs. "She was. Until the day Dad announced he had to go to Italy, on location. That set her off."

"Why can't he take her?" I ask.

"He offered, but she refuses to go. I can't understand her. No one can when she gets like this. Anyway, when Dad brought up the idea of the clinic, Mom freaked. She said, 'I'm just a social drinker' — but she could barely get the words out, and she was banging into furniture. <u>In the middle of the day!"</u>

I tell Maggie things will work out. I remind her how far <u>she's</u> come with her problems.

This is so sad, Nbook. Maggie's trying not to cry. <u>I'm</u> trying not to cry. Just then, two hands reach around my head and cover my eyes. "Don't even try to get away," says a deep voice.

"Hi, Ducky," I say. (He's a worse actor than I am.)

He's with Sunny. They're escaping Dawn. They're planning some kind of good-bye celebration for her. (She goes back to Connecticut to stay with her mom every summer.)

As they tell us about it, I watch Maggie. Her eyes are dry. She seems psyched, and she asks about the date of the party.

Ducky shrugs. "Don't know yet."

"Where's it going to be?" I ask.

"Don't know," Ducky replies. "We're just at the talking stage."

"She's not leaving for Connecticut for two weeks," Sunny says.

Sunny and Ducky start throwing out suggestions for the party. (I'm thinking: Connecticut . . . that's close to western Massachusetts, right?)

Anyway, they can't agree on anything.

Finally Maggie puts in her two cents — have the party at Ducky's. His parents are still in Ghana, so there will be "no permission problems."

Brilliant idea. Ducky and Sunny agree.
And then:

She answers. It's her dad. He wants her to come home and convince Mrs. Blume to listen to him.
Maggie says no, she's already agreed to stay for dinner — and for the night — at my house.

So here we are, in my room. Maggie's asleep in a sleeping bag on the floor, twisting and turning.
And I'm finally tired.
Much more to say.
Mañana.

OK, I didn't tell you what happened after Maggie and I got home last night.

It's almost dinnertime. Maggie goes to the bathroom to wash up. Papi's standing in the front hall with the phone notepad in his hand. On it are two words:

— Brendan

— Brendan

"He called twice," Papi says.

I thank him and take the sheet.

He's standing there, not moving aside. "How's your homework going?"

"Fine," I say.

"You're going to be prepared for finals?"

"Hope so."

Now Mami comes into the hall. She's got a warm, patient smile. She asks about our afternoon, then says, "Brendan seems like a nice boy."

I can see where this is leading. "He's just a good friend," I say.

Isabel, studying in the den, has a sudden coughing fit.

"You know, Amalia," Mami says, "Finals are coming up."

"What does Brendan have to do with finals?"

"You do seem to be spending an awful lot of time with him," Papi says.

"It's not <u>studying</u> time, though," I reply.

Now Isabel sounds like she's dying of pneumonia.

"<u>Will you knock it off?</u>" I yell out.

"We don't mean to pressure you, hija," Mami says. "We love your friends, all of them. And we don't mind that Maggie comes over here so much. She's like one of the family. We know what she's going through. But between her and Brendan . . . well, I just want to be sure you have enough time for <u>Amalia</u>."

"In a few weeks the summer will be here," Papi says. "And you'll have all the free time in the world."

"I know that!" I reply. "A whole, free, boring summer."

They're just staring at me, wondering why I said that.

When Maggie emerges, I disappear upstairs.

They don't need to know what's on my mind.

I can't even figure it out.

Tuesday, 6/1
Lunch

Maggie comes over after school. Around dinnertime, we're trying to do hwork on the front porch, but mainly just talking.

Brendan rides by on his bike. Like, oh, I just happened to turn down Royal Lane, what a surprise.

We chat. He says, "Hey, maybe we can all go out Friday."

Maggie tells him that Tyler has to be in L.A. for an interview.

But I say yes.

I wasn't going to study Friday night anyway.

Depressing Item #1: Today Ms. Fong assigns us a report on <u>1984</u>. She assumes we've all read it, since it's on our reading list.

Wrong.

Plus, she announces the final is going to be all essay questions —

chosen at random from any of the topics we've studied all year. But she won't say exactly <u>which</u> topics or which books. So we have to know <u>everything.</u>

Depressing Item #2: I skip lunch to meet with Ms. Sevekow about math. She explains everything. Patiently. At least three times.

I am starting to understand stuff that confused me in September.

Only eight more months to go.

Depressing Item #3: On the way to study hall, I turn the corner and see Amanda Janson talking to Dawn.

Taking a break from <u>1984</u>.

Got 2 write fast. Isabel & I taking turns on phone. Rite now she's dealing w/ rental car probl. I'm supposed to call Robinsons'. The nite b4 big anniv. party, Robnsns r taking Mami & Papi to M's college reunion in San Diego. Will stay overnite & return in time for party.

OK, Dawn-party update:

Sunny's furious about Amanda's big mouth. Says we HAVE to change our plans. And if Dawn suspects anything, DENY, DENY, DENY.

Ducky's cool. Says we can plan something else.

So S & D are coming over tonight.

So's Maggie. Again.

Says she wants to do homework. (Which is what she said yesterday.) Anyway, now she'll help with party plans.

Then she can give me a summary of <u>1984</u>.

Her dad probably worked on the movie.

Maggie stays for dinner. Leaves at 9:30. Saint Isabel says, "Things must be bad at her house. These days, it feels like she lives here."

You know what? I hate to say this (and don't you _dare_ tell anyone I did), but she has a point. It _does_ feel like Maggie lives here.

I love Maggie, Nbook. I understand her problems. As far as I'm concerned, mi casa es su casa. (Plus, she did help me with 1984 and math.)

But let's face it, Maggie _does_ have a casa of her own. Running away from her problems isn't going to help. Sooner or later she has to face up to them.

I sure learned that the hard way. If I hadn't faced up to James, he'd _still_ be harassing me.

Oh, well. Must be hard for her. I mean, she's been working so hard on her eating disorder with Dr. Fuentes. I

guess a person can only handle
one major crisis at a time, huh,
Nbook?

Anyway, as we're getting ready for
bed, I casually mention to Mami and
Papi that Brendan asked me to go out
with him on Friday.

Papi says, "It's almost the week of
finals."

I say, "It's the Friday <u>before</u> the
week <u>before</u> finals."

Mami and Papi agree to think about
the date — if I promise I'll study all
weekend long.

Oh. P.S.

1. Isabel talked to Mr. Robinson. He
says everything's cool with the San
Diego trip.

2. All the relatives have confirmed.

3. You'll never guess what Ducky
and Sunny decided on for Dawn's party.
Bowling.

Maybe this time Tyler will wear a
disguise.

11:43

can't. sleep.

Thursday, 6/3
social studies

Finals begin a week from Monday.
11 days.

On the way to school today I'm thinking about this and freaking out. Suddenly the Winslows' car zooms by. Going 60, at least. Stops in front of school. Sunny jumps out and slams the door. Car zooms off with a squeal of tires.

I jog over to her and ask what's up.

"Dad's mad at Mom," she says.

"Mad? But — she's . . ."

"Dead? I know that. That's even more reason for him to be mad. She can't talk back. Dad likes a one-sided fight."

(Sometimes, Nbook, talking to Sunny is like being splashed with very cold water.)

I just nod.

"He's mad at me for not being her," she goes on. "He's mad that I'm not old enough to run his bookstore. He's mad at the bookstore for not doing better business. He's mad at just about everyone in Palo City for not reading more books. Any other questions?"

Actually, yes.

"Does he want to hire me?" I ask.

Sunny does a double take. "Are you serious?"

"If Ducky can do it —"

"Ducky's 16."

"So I'll work fewer hours. Whatever is legal. Or I'll volunteer. It'd give me something to do. I can read books about art."

Sunny smiles. "Or travel. There are lots of books about Massachusetts. . . ."

5:01

I can go.

On the date tomorrow, that is.

If I study like crazy tonight. And after school tomorrow before the date. And over the weekend.

'Bye, Nbook. No offense.

Time to

Friday, 6/4
5:3¢

I'm on a roll, Nbook.

I do all the math section reviews up until February.

I call Marina, who faxes me a bunch of notes from English class.

I start <u>The Good Earth</u>, the book, which I should have read but never did because I rented the movie. (The book's better.)

Now I'm waiting for Isabel. She's painting her face for <u>her</u> date with SBTLB. (Mami made her promise to drive me and Brendan to the movie theater, which may explain the huffing and puffing noises in the bathroom.)

No matter. I feel so much better, Nbook.

This all may work out.

OK, I think I see him down the block.

Later.

~~I~~
~~I wasn't~~
~~I want to~~
~~WHO DO THEY THINK~~

Can't
write

My face is corroding.

That's what it feels like, Nbook. I know it's not true and I've washed it ten times BUT THAT'S WHAT IT FEELS LIKE. Right at that spot on the left cheek where she spit at me.

Why?
WHY?
What did I do, Nbook? WHAT DID I
DO?

Got to think straight. My head is
splitting apart.
OK, slow down.
Start at the beginning.
It hurts to think about the
beginning — because it was so
wonderful, Nbook. We walk into Café
Con Leche, and André makes me feel
like his favorite customer. Romantic
booth. Free appetizers. Treats
Brendan like a son. Doggie bag full of
pastries, on the house.
At the cineplex, the usher knows
we have food but doesn't stop us. The
movie's much better than I expect it
to be. And Brendan is so nice. He
puts his arm around my shoulder — the
right way too. Doesn't keep it there
for two hours like a cement drainpipe,
the way Danny Cruz did in San Diego.
And he doesn't wait for _me_ to laugh

before he laughs (which Danny also did).

Anyway, I feel us kind of melting together. Like a couple, Nbook. Like I finally, really want us to be a couple — because I trust him.

Toward the end of the movie he leans over toward me — gently, easily — and I can tell he wants to kiss me, but it doesn't feel awkward or pressured, and I know that if I just keep looking at the screen he'll turn away and it'll be OK, he'll understand. But I don't want to turn away — he's so tender and handsome, and our kiss lasts just the right amount of time — and when it's over I feel thrilled. Afterward, he doesn't act all weird, like now our faces should be welded together at the lips for the rest of the movie. We sit back, arms around each other, relaxed and happy.

We leave the cineplex, arm in arm. Isabel's not there yet, but that's OK because the night is clear and cool. I know nothing bad is going to happen. I'm _safe_ with him. He's no James.

People are flowing out of the theater, splitting off in various directions, until we're the only ones left standing in front. Soon the usher starts to lock the door, but Brendan runs to her and convinces her to let him use the rest room.

As he goes inside, the usher asks if I want to wait in the lobby. I say no thanks. I want to smell the blossoms, not stale popcorn.

So I stay outside, breathing the sweet air, looking up the street for Isabel's car. I figure she's probably having a great time too, which means she'll be late and maybe Brendan and I can hang out at the ice-cream shop.

I'm not sure if the shop is open. It looks like its lights are off. So I'm squinting, trying to see it clearer, when I hear voices behind me — girls' voices. None of them sound familiar, so I don't bother looking back. Half of them are laughing, drowning out the words of the others.

Like someone has just reached into me and ripped out my soul. The usher is talking to me, asking questions, but I don't hear her. I am not thinking in words. I am seeing red and black. I want to run after those girls and pull out their hair, throw them against the brick wall, make them feel how I feel.

But they're far away now, weaving down the street — fast. They're laughing and slapping each other five. They're not even looking back over their shoulders. It's like I don't exist. I was a game. A distraction.

To them, I am not even a person.

And then suddenly I see

All I can think is <u>what took you so long? Where were you?</u> But I don't say it.

He and the woman help me up. I try to tell them what happened, but I can't. I'm bad enough with words to begin with. Now they're all slipping and sliding out of my mouth with no sense.

The worst part is the spit. I mean, I'm not normally grossed out by blood or body fluids. But when I felt that spit on my cheek I almost threw up.

It's not the saliva. It's what it means. Spit is a waste product. It belongs in a toilet or a sink — or the gutter or a sewer. Not on a human being's face.

It feels like it's still there, Nbook. Like I'll never get it off.

Saturday, 6/5
6:17 A.M.

Isn't this the worst irony? I finally crash at 2 and now I'm up again, raring to go.

My nightgown is soaked. I wake up in a sweat. I'm dreaming I'm in Dr. Fuentes's office but my hair is dyed blonde and I'm slapping thick base on my face. Very light base. The girls from last night are looking at me through a two-way mirror and laughing like crazy. I can hear them and so can Dr. F but I put on the makeup anyway.

It's a dream, it's not real, I remind myself.

I wish all of last night were a dream, Nbook. I could forget about it then. But it's stuck in my brain, and I can't stop thinking of those faces, those leering faces looking at me like I'm some _thing_, like an old shoe or a dead pigeon.

I don't look at anyone like that. Do I? No one's supposed to treat another person that way.

What did I do? What did I say? WHY DO I KEEP ASKING THAT?

I didn't do anything. I was there, that's all.

I was Latina. I am Latina.

I mean, yeah, OK, this stuff happens. I know that, Nbook. I'm not stupid. My eyes and ears are open. I read papers and magazines and I watch the news. The reminders are all around, every week. The way Papi is treated sometimes by the people at his company. The way that patient of Mami's sneered and said, "Vargas? I thought that was Italian," and never came for a second session. And all the other small, daily stuff at Vista like the girls who talk one way with white girls and a whole other way with me. The jokes that suddenly get cut off when someone sees me.

It's bad. It's wrong. But you live with it. What else can you do? You tell people when it bothers you. You love your family and friends, you do your best, and you realize the world ain't perfect and never will be. That's all any of us can do.

<u>I know that.</u>

But they spat on me, Nbook.

They knocked me down and spat on me and walked away.

And they were proud of it.

Then what? What do they do when they get home? Brag to their moms and dads? "Well, let's see, we went out and had a really good pizza with pepperoni, saw a great movie, beat up this wetback, and stopped in at the ice-cream shop." Is that what they do?

Got to calm down & try to figure this out.

Got to leave this bedroom. Go to a new place where I can think better. Hang on.

That's better.

No one's up. Isabel's making a funny noise in her sleep. Kind of a whimper-snore. Guess her dreams aren't so terrific either.

OK, I said I'd try to figure this out. Which means writing about what else happened last night.

I don't want to, Nbook — but if I don't, it'll just feel worse.

Be glad you're not a human being. It's hard.

Anyway . . .

My legs are shaking as I leave the women's room. Walking in I'd been straight and steady, but walking out I'm like jelly.

The usher — _What was her name, Nbook? I wish I remembered!_ — she sits me down and gives me a soft drink and some candy. I drink but I have no appetite.

I can't sit still for long and I'm dying to get out of there, out of that neighborhood, out of town. I want to crawl into the backseat of a car and ride and ride for weeks without stopping.

That's when we hear a loud knock. It's Isabel, pressing her face to the glass door of the cineplex, looking all worried and guilty about being late. Simon is behind her.

I don't know why I'm not mad at them. I should be. If they'd been there on time, none of this would have happened. But I'm just so happy to see her. I jump out of my seat and run to the door. The usher opens it, and I fly into my sister's arms.

"What happened?" she asks.

I'm sobbing. My eyes are soaking Isabel's new white cotton blouse, but she doesn't yell at me, she just calmly strokes my hair, the way she did when I was little. "Just take me home," is all I manage to say.

The usher is pretty wet-eyed too. She stuffs a couple of free movie passes into Brendan's hand. "For another night," she says, "on me. And you look after her."

In the car, I sit in the backseat. Brendan tries to put his arm around me but I push it aside. I don't feel like being touched right at that moment. I tell Isabel the whole ordeal — and this time I'm making more sense.

She listens and listens. When I get to the part about the spitting, suddenly she steers over to the side of the road and stops.

The tears convince her, I guess. We drive home, almost totally silent. Brendan tries to put his arm around me again, and this time I let him. He doesn't say much, but I guess that's OK. It's important to know how to be quiet with someone. You know what I mean, Nbook.

Frankly, it feels good to be held. Just held.

Isabel drops off Brendan first. He says a quiet, gentle good-bye. Then we drop off Simon. He's sweet, reassuring me, telling me that the girls were sick and strung out on alcohol, that I shouldn't take it personally, that if I ever see another one of those girls, just let him know and he'll make her life miserable.

Now I'm alone with Isabel.

She's driving way too fast. She's muttering angrily, using words I wouldn't dare repeat on your pages, Nbook.

She is so upset that she runs a red light. Right through it. I mean, if

another car had been coming along,
we'd be dead meat.

"WHAT ARE YOU DOING?" I scream.

"Sorry," Isabel mutters.

"Can't you slow down? What are
you angry about?"

"I'm angry about those girls."

"It didn't happen to _you_."

"You're my sister."

My heart is thumping. I shut up so
she can concentrate. We both fall into
kind of an exhausted silence.

As we pull up to the house, only
the porch and front-room lights are on.
Mami and Papi's bedroom is dark.

I feel relieved. I don't want to
talk about what happened. I don't
want to get them upset. All I want to
do is go right to sleep, clothes and all.

I stumble into the house behind
Isabel. But she's running toward the
stairs, shouting, "Mami? Are you still
awake?"

I chase after her. "Don't! Isabel,
they don't need to know about this!"

Isabel looks at me as if I'm nuts. "Amalia, you can't just let this drop."

"It's not that big a deal —"

"It was a <u>huge</u> deal. Those girls were racist!"

"They were drinking. They didn't know what they were doing. They probably won't even remember what happened by tomorrow morning."

"So what? What's that got to do with it?"

She pulls away and races upstairs. I sink into a kitchen chair and fiddle with a napkin. My hands are shaking and I can't control them.

I realize I'm <u>embarrassed</u>, Nbook. I feel like a little kid who did something wrong. Like I shouldn't be there in the kitchen, all dirty and beaten up. If I'd done the right thing — gone into the cineplex instead of staying outside, or fought back better, or run away, anything but what I ended up doing, <u>which was nothing</u> — I'd be fine.

Of course Mami and Papi come running down the stairs to see if I'm all right. And I start crying all over again.

I expect them to get angry or worked up, but they don't. They just hold me and comfort me. Papi starts asking about the girls, what they looked like, etc. I try to answer, but I get about as far as the part where they called me names, and I start to break down.

He just backs off, holding me and saying he's glad I'm home. "You used good sense," he says. "The worst thing would have been to try to fight back."

"You're here," Mami says. "You're safe. You're still you."

"And we love you," Papi adds.

I sob and sob. And all I can think is, <u>I DID try to fight back. I could have gotten myself hurt. AM I CRAZY?</u>

OK. Sorry, Nbook, I have to stop. My fingers are cramped and my head hurts. Maybe I'll go back to bed.

I wake up with my heart pounding. It's 9:30. I've only been asleep a few minutes. It feels like a whole day has gone by.

I go to the kitchen, feeling spooked. Isabel is eating cereal and reading a magazine. I say hi but it comes out a grunt.

"You look awful." She puts down her magazine and frowns at me. "You didn't sleep well, did you?"

I shake my head.

"You know, you really should have called the police."

"Maybe."

"If it were me, I'd be at the station house all night if I had to. Then, when they caught those animals, I'd march over to their houses and spit in their faces."

Right.

I ignore her. I look in the cupboards, but nothing interests me.

Now Papi's shuffling into the kitchen in his pj's and robe. "Hey, who wants frittatas?" he calls out.

"I already ate," Isabel says.

"No, thanks," I say.

Papi pats my shoulder and asks me if I'm OK. I say yes, but I don't fool him. "Sit," he says. "Relax. These'll be so good you won't be able to resist."

I try to have an appetite. I tell myself how much I love Papi's frittatas. And he really does them up. He's throwing in green peppers and cheese and spices, dancing and singing.

But my stomach is like a tight fist. Thinking about food, I feel nauseated.

I get up from the table, just as Mami comes down to the kitchen. She tells me that Ducky and Maggie both called while I was out last night. She apologizes for not mentioning it.

Under the circumstances, I totally understand.

I want to call them. But I can't.

Maybe later.

7:01 P.M.

Still haven't called.

Can't move.

Feeling really tired. Didn't do much today except go shopping with Isabel.

I didn't want to go. Didn't want to leave the house.

I am so totally not excited about this party now. Don't know why.

Anyway, Isabel and I go to Leo's and order food for the party. After

we're done, outside the store, Isabel
suddenly grabs my arm. She's looking
at a girl across the street. She says,
"Is <u>that</u> one of them?"

My heart starts pounding — literally.
I can feel my shirt moving.

I can't tell if the girl is one of my
attackers. She might be. I kind of
stutter and say I don't know, and the
girl's already halfway down the block.

Isabel seems impatient. "You can't
be scared of them, you know. They
feed off the fear."

Before this, I am feeling fine. But
now, as we get into the car, I'm
paranoid.

i tell you, Amalia, if
I had been there
with you...

Next we stop off at Winslow Books.

Isabel wants this book about party planning.

While she's looking, I spot the travel section. There are no books about western Massachusetts but plenty about New England. So I pick one up. And as I'm reading, I see

Suddenly I feel like I'm going to throw up. I go to the bathroom.

I'm hanging over the sink and the nausea's slowly going away — and soon Isabel's inside, looking at me like I'm insane.

I tell her why I'm there. Her eyes flare. And she marches out of the bathroom.

This is awful, Nbook. So
embarrassing.

Why did this have to happen now?

Why did this have to happen at
all?

I have to study.

Maybe tomorrow I'll feel better.

It's late.
Can't sleep. Again.
Every time I feel myself drifting off, I go

Oh. Guess who's fast asleep on my floor right now?

How, you may be wondering, did this happen?

She phones around 8 P.M. She asks why I haven't returned her calls.

I remind her she only called once. She replies, "Isn't that enough?"

She's in a foul mood. She launches into this speech about how much she hates the movie business. Why? Because Tyler's going away on location for three weeks — to replace another actor who backed out of a movie. Turns out he <u>knew</u> he might have to do this, but he didn't mention it to Maggie until last night — over the phone! She feels totally betrayed.

So what does she do? Hangs up on him and yells at her dad.

Naturally he yells back. Then she tells him he doesn't understand. And he storms away.

Life at the Blumes'.

Anyway, she's mad at the world. And she wants to come over here.

"Sure," I say.

"And how was your date?" she finally asks.

"I got beaten up," I reply.

Long silence. "You _what_?"

I go through the whole story. I hear her muttering "Oh my God" every few seconds.

I'm exhausted when I finish. I'm crying. She's crying too. She says she'll be right over.

Right over means an hour later — in Ducky's car, with Sunny. Yes, she's called and told them everything (Dawn knows too, but she wasn't home).

Maggie has flowers. Sunny has ice cream. Ducky has a CD.

I feel like it's my birthday.

Sunny and Ducky want to hear what happened, so I tell them. Maggie holds my hand. She says it's good to talk these things out. It makes you feel better.

Fat chance. It feels just as horrible the third time as it did the first. But I guess it is nice to have friends around. At least when you cry you're not the only one.

Eventually Ducky manages to change the subject. He has an update on the Dawn party.

Friday in school Sunny started stressing over the bowling party (she says it's because she's never bowled — Ducky says she's worried about her nails), so they were talking about it in the school hallway, hidden away near the custodial office.

So . . . there's a new plan now — an ocean dinner cruise.

OK, Nbook, I'm feeling a little better.
It's 2:17.
Time to sign off and try to sleep.
Wish me luck.

Sunday, 6/6
8:1ϕ A.M.

Did it.

More or less.

Bad dreams again. Don't want to write about them.

Maggie still asleep. Hasn't moved.

12:35

When Maggie finally wakes up this morning, she's alert and cheery. I'm a dishrag.

We eat breakfast (well, she does).

We try to study (well, she does).

I can't concentrate at all. Too tired to focus, too wired to sleep.

She keeps asking if I'm OK — if I'm still thinking about the "incident." That's what she calls it.

I can't bear to talk about it. I change the subject and ask about Tyler.

Her face tightens. She's still mad

at him, for many reasons. I hear all
of them.

Soon Dawn comes over. She brings
me a big white floppy hat, some
homemade pie, and photos of Gracie. I
feel like someone recovering from
some illness in a hospital.

Of course _she_ needs to hear
everything. This time it's not so easy to
change topics.

She's sympathetic.

I'm just pathetic.

I try to be a good friend. I try to
let her cheer me up. But I feel
nothing.

Around noon, Reg picks up Maggie.
Takes Dawn too.

Alone again.

Back to the books.

7:30 P.M.

The mice are attacking, Nbook.
At least that's what it sounds like.

While Mami and Papi are at a church meeting, Isabel's trying to do a high-speed cassette dub — the best hits of Tito Puente, Celia Cruz, all the good old stuff that the relatives like.

Tomorrow after school we're shopping for party goods. Then we'll hide them at Simon's.

I should be so excited about this party.

I'm not.

What will the neighbors think?

What are we doing, Nbook?
Is this party a good idea?
Here? In Palo City?

Why are we asking people we love to come to a place like this — a place where you can't even stand on a public sidewalk without being assaulted?

I've learned something, Nbook. I've learned I'm a fool.

I trusted too much. I let myself be a target.

I didn't realize that people will hate you for no good reason, and you can't control it. It doesn't matter who you are, how you dress, what you sound like, what's in your brain.

It's how you look. Period.

And if you run into people whose minds work that way, ain't nothing you can do.

So my question to you today, Nbook, is, How many of them are in Palo City? Is it 5%? 20%? 75%?

Are those girls the only ones, the only racists in Palo City?

Yeah. Right.

They had to get their attitudes from somewhere — parents, brothers, sisters, friends. Anti-Latino sites on the Web. Whatever.

It took me awhile to realize how bad it is. But now I know. It can happen anywhere, anytime.

How long will it take for it to happen to Abuela Aurora? Or Hector or Cristina?

Maybe while they're walking through the airport.

Maybe on Sunday morning, when Abuela takes her traditional walk to the bakery for fresh rolls.

I have this creepy feeling, Nbook, that we should cancel.

9:17

Nguyen.
Asami.
Jose.
Kareem.
Asif.
Luis.
Benazir.

Do you know who these people are, Nbook? They are characters in the math word problems.

Now, I never really noticed these names before. But today I do. And I think, Hmm, the writers are really trying to make people of color feel included.

"People of color." Those are the exact words that pop into my head.

And here's what I realize: That is the world's stupidest expression.

What does it mean anyway? Of color compared to whom? Who isn't of color? Everyone I know is — brown, tan, pink, yellow, olive, beige.

OK, Nbook, you're not "of color." Your pages are white.

And that, dear Notebook, is the real answer. "Of color" means "not white."

Think about it. It means we Latinos are defined by what we're not.

But who is white?

Those girls at the theater — they're white. At least in their own minds. This obviously means a lot to them. "Of color," to them, translates as "different." Which, I guess, is a short jump from "bad" and "threatening."

But this is what I just don't get. Threatening to <u>what</u>? Who could be threatened by <u>me</u>?

Correct me if I'm wrong, Nbook, but I was born in America, right? And that makes me an American citizen. Which means I can go to their schools, shop at their stores, see their movies, stand on their sidewalks without fear of being attacked for the way I look.

<u>MY</u> schools. <u>MY</u> stores. <u>MY</u> sidewalks. They're mine too.

The truth is, if Maggie had been standing in front of the theater the other night, those girls would have passed right by.

This is what Maggie can't understand — I mean, <u>really</u> understand. In her soul. Or Dawn or Sunny or Brendan or CeCe or Marina. Maybe Ducky, a little bit. The boys make fun of him for being different — but that's just because of his mannerisms and the way he dresses and the fact that he hates sports.

Now, I love Maggie. She knows it too, otherwise she wouldn't be over here so often. She feels the warmth and closeness in our family. She wishes she were in our family. And she is, in a way.

But she could never know what it is like to be a Vargas. She has something none of us have. She is <u>wealthy</u>. She is <u>white</u>. And what happened to me will never, ever happen to her in her life.

Nbook, I can't believe I just wrote that.

Midnight

Yes, I can.
It's the truth.

Sooooooooo tired.

Just read over the last 2 entries. They give me a queasy feeling.

But I can't think about it now. Have to learn about the Krebs cycle.

Nbook, I wish there were no such thing as the Krebs cycle. It looks like this:

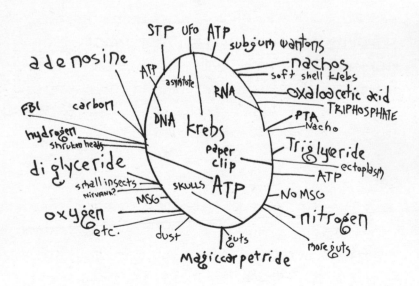

Sorry, Nbook. Ms. DePhillipis caught me. She says, "Oh, have you discovered some hidden depths to the Krebs cycle?"

I say, "No comprendo Eenglees."

(Just kidding about that last part.)

What is with Brendan?

He's in homeroom. He looks at me. Nods. But he splits at the sound of the bell.

OK, fine, I figure he has something important to do.

Which is too bad. After class, Cece wants to know what happened on the date. As I'm telling her, I feel I could use some moral support.

Then, at lunch, I see Brendan sitting at another table, clear across the room. I look at him. He looks back. Then his eyes dart away.

I don't get it.

OK, Vargas, calm down. It's the last week of school. Maybe Brendan just wants to be with his friends before heading off to East Neptune for the summer.

Or maybe he has realized for the first time that I'm Latina.

Maybe they don't have Mexicans where he grew up in New Jersey.

8:31 P.M.

Remind me not to talk, Nbook. Remind me I shouldn't open my big mouth to anyone until finals are over.

I can't believe myself after school today.

I know. I'm a jerk.
I'll call her.

9:27 P.M.

When I call, Zeke picks up the
phone. He says, "Let me see if she
wants to speak to you."

Not a good sign.

Maggie doesn't pick up for a long
time. When she finally does, her voice
is like this:

I tell her I'm sorry. I explain that I'm really behind in studying, that I'm still kind of shook up about Friday night, yada yada yada.

When I finish, she says, "I'm really not trying to be part of your family."

"I know you're not," I reply.

"You can come over to my house if you want. We don't always have to go to yours."

"Thanks."

"How about tomorrow?"

"I have to go shopping with Isabel."

Long, long silence. "OK, fine. 'Bye."

Now I feel worse. Like I just blew the whole friendship. Like, if I hang up now, it's adiós amiga.

I need all the friends I can get, Nbook.

So I quickly say, "No, wait. I'll come over Wednesday. You can coach me on the math."

"You don't have to if you don't want to," Maggie replies.

"It's OK. I want to."
"Uh-huh. See you then."

She hates me.

Tuesday, 6/8
Homeroom

Leavitt's in a bad mood. We're supposed to be studying. Don't want him to catch me. Will make this fast.

Bad dreams last night. Again. Woke up at 3 A.M. and couldn't go back to sleep. The scene outside the theater again — only the girls have changed. They're Maggie and Sunny and Dawn and Cece and Marina.

I try to run away, but I'm pushed back from the other side — by my dear sister, Isabel. She's telling me I shouldn't <u>dare</u> run away. I should face up to them.

I'm up shaking until breakfast.

When I finally stagger downstairs
for breakfast, Isabel

Sorry about that.

Leavitt trouble.

I'm innocently writing and Mr. Leavitt
turns around and says, "Writing fan mail
to Short Hills?" He calls Brendan "Short
Hills" because that's his hometown
(and because that's the kind of guy
Mr. Leavitt is).

Ignore him. Back to Isabel. This
morning.

Number 1. She knows I have
insomnia.

Number 2. She knows I've been
having nightmares.

Number 3. She can tell by my
face that it's been a hard night.

So what does she do? (a) Offer to
make me breakfast and give me a
shoulder rub? (b) Sit me down and

say with a smile, "Do you want to talk about it?" or (c) shake her head and say, "Just remember, they're laughing right now. They're waking up all fresh and happy, and they're saying, 'What other Latina can we spit on today?' You can still call the police, you know. It'll make you feel better."

(c), of course.

I cannot even answer.

I turn, go back to my room, get dressed, and leave for school. I don't even say good morning to Mami and Papi.

I'm still furious.

And I'm starving.

Study hall

Where am I, Nbook?

Did I take a wrong turn and end up in some parallel dimension where everyone looks exactly like the people I know but with defective personalities?

I mean, Isabel the witch sister is bad enough. But now it's the Un-Brendan.

Four days ago he's fun and comfortable and funny. Just about perfect.

Ever since Friday night — when I needed him the most — he's a pod person. This is his range of reactions to me:

I say hi and he gives me this funny look. I walk to classes with him and he hardly says a word.

I <u>think</u> he's still my friend. He doesn't run away or yell at me. He

doesn't seem mad. But what is he
thinking? Is he still feeling bad about
Friday night? Does he hate me?
    What did I do?

                            After school
                    Waiting for Isabel . . .
    Am I nuts? Why do I obsess about
him? I'M the one I should be
obsessing about.
    Besides, what's the point of getting
involved with someone who's about to
leave for the whole summer?

Sorry about that, Nbook. Don't worry,
we're alone again. Isabel's late.

First, an explanation for above:

Roll the time back, to sixth period
today. Ducky's late for gym (as usual,
gossiping with Dawn and Sunny too long).
He races through the hallway, but
some Cro Mag knocks him down
accidentally-on-purpose. His books spill
all over the place.

Sunny and Dawn rush over to help.

Anyway, they both corner me right after science and tell me what happened. I tell them they should go ahead and have the cruise anyway.

I tell them no, not yet. We say good-bye.

But here's the weird thing, Nbook. Here's the thing that makes me think I am seriously disturbed.

As I'm leaving, I'm starting to cry. I'm feeling <u>jealous</u>.

Maybe it's just my weird frame of mind. Maybe it's because my relationships are falling apart all around me. Maybe it's because those two make such a cute couple.

I mean, they're perfect together.

SUNNY	DUCKY
tough	good-natured
insecure	level-headed
nice underneath it all	nice above all
fun to be with	fun to be with
dealing with mom's death	dealing with Alex's suicide attempt

OK, so what? Why feel jealous?

Because <u>they</u> have what it takes, Nbook. Not Brendan and me.

Because I'm thinking, maybe he finally woke up and saw how different we are.

If you know what I mean . . .

Oh, god. Listen to me.

WHERE IS ISABEL?

In the car now. Going home. How was shopping?
Can.
Barely.
Hold.
My.
Pen.

Wednesday, 6/9
Lunch

Foul mood.
Nothing good to say.
Nothing to say at all.

6:11 P.M.

MAGGIE BLUME IS HISTORY.

I give her the benefit of the doubt. I <u>help</u> her. I take her seriously through all her problems. What does she do for <u>me</u>? Who does she think I am?

Chill, Amalia. Slow down.

OK, Nbook, you want to know what happened? Here's what happened.

We're in Maggie's room, studying. The Great and Powerful Hayden Blume is actually home. Well, sort of. His ear is grafted to a cell phone, so he's running around the house giving orders to people who aren't there.

Next thing you know, he's knocking on Maggie's door.

He peeks in. Just wants to say hi. And then . . .

Those are just about the last
words we say to each other, Nbook.
And as far as I'm con

Oh, Nbook.
My head is reeling.
I think I am losing it.
Maybe I did lose it already.
First of all, about the last entry —
it was Isabel who rudely interrupted
us . . .

What she went through?

She never went through anything, I'm thinking.

At least she never told me.

So I ask her what's the matter.

"Remember my birthday party last year in San Diego?" she says.

How can I forget? She and her friends went out to a dance — and when she came home she wouldn't talk to us. She went right to her room and slammed the door.

I thought she was just being snotty. Or she was upset about leaving her boyfriend, Greg, to move here.

It's more than that.

ISABEL'S STORY

Nbook, this is so unlike my sister.

Our house was <u>miles</u> from Club Mazatlan. She never told us she'd walked. She never told us a thing.

"Isabel," I say, "you should have said something."

My sister's eyes are moist. "I wish I could go back. If I could do it all over again, I would have made a scene, right in the café. I would have given them a piece of my mind. I dream about that night all the time. I replay it over and over. <u>Now</u> do you see why I'm bugging you? It's bad enough to live through something like that — but it was even worse to see my little sister go through the same thing. <u>I just don't want you to suffer the way I did, Amalia.</u>"

So that's it, Nbook. <u>That's</u> why she's been so impossible. She thinks she's protecting me.

"Isabel," I say, "what happened to me was different."

"In a way. But those girls <u>won</u>, Amalia. They just walked away without paying a price — the way those kids at the café won."

"They didn't win anything. Someday they will pay."

"What good will that do us?"

"Isabel, it's over. It happened. Okay, maybe you could have done something different. Maybe you're not perfect. Why stay so angry? That's exactly what they would have wanted. It's like you're <u>letting</u> them win."

"Because they destroyed a piece of me, right in front of my friends. They took away my dignity, same as those girls did to you. It's too late for me to do anything, but you can fight back —"

"Your dignity is <u>inside</u> you, Isabel. You still have it, no matter what those jerks said."

"I don't really believe that," Isabel snaps, getting up from the bed. "Do you?"

Do I, Nbook?

I say nothing to Isabel as she leaves.

Because I don't know.

Sleep time
(Right.)

AMALIA'S DILEMMA, AS SEEN BY ISABEL

WHAT IS WRONG WITH THIS PICTURE?

I see it, Nbook.

It's clear now.

Yeah, those girls were awful. They took a part of me, turned it inside out, and then left without looking back. And I let them go.

But what exactly did they take with them?

Not Amalia.

I'm still here. Still the same girl.

They took their hate. And it's still inside them. It's curdling and rotting away — always hungry, always needing to be fed.

OK, they got away with it this time. But that kind of hunger is never satisfied. It'll act up again. And someday they'll pay for it.

I don't need to hate them back.

I don't need to feel bitter either. Or sorry for myself.

Those feelings curdle your insides too.

I know what you're thinking, Nbook: Don't be stupid. Don't turn your back to trouble.

I am wiser now. My eyes are wide open. I will sense danger better. I promise.

But I can't stop living. I can't stop being me.

What I told Isabel was right,
Nbook. I have my dignity.
No one can touch it.
I am not a balloon, dear sister.
My holes heal.

Thursday morning, 6/1∅
Before school

AMALIA'S DREAM

It's over, Nbook. It really is. I <u>feel</u> it. Those horrible girls are gone. They're not floating around in my brain anymore, laughing at me like evil spirits.

It was Isabel who got me through this, really. I mean, not the way she <u>thought</u> she would. Not by badgering me. By opening up — finally — and making me see the answer myself. I guess I helped her as much as she helped me.

That's what sisters are for, huh, Nbook?

So this morning I feel like a human again. Sunny tells me we're going to kidnap Dawn to the beach on the Friday after finals (exactly the way Sunny wanted it in the first place) — and I actually feel excited about this.

I have my life again. Which is great.

The life that I have, unfortunately, is a disaster.

Forget about Brendan. I can barely remember what his face looks like, but I know every contour of his back. I've seen much more of it than I'd like this week. His brain is probably halfway to Massachusetts already.

I want to talk to him, Nbook. But I don't know what to say. Why is he so silent? I wish I knew how he felt about me.

I wish I knew how I felt about him.

Maggie? I'll be lucky if I get the evil eye from her. I may have really blown it with her.

Time for Project Rescue Me.

OK, Amalia. It's up to you, girl.

If you want 'em, go get 'em.

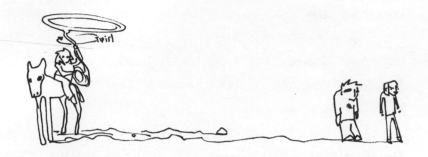

After hroom I'm talking to Cece in the hallway, when Brendan comes up to me.

Cece gives me a look and shoots away. Brendan hands me three pages, neatly folded.

I unfold them and see they're computer-printed in this tiny font. And they begin with "Dear Amalia."

I say, "What's this?" Like, I'm supposed to <u>read</u> the whole thing right there? It would take me until lunch.

He fidgets and shrugs. He says it's an apology for leaving me outside the theater. For not being there when those girls came. For letting me get beaten up.

He's mad at himself. Embarrassed too, for being so helpless that night. <u>That's</u> why he hasn't been talking to me.

I can't believe what I'm hearing. All this time wasted, all this worrying — because of <u>this</u>? Because he blames himself for something that has nothing to do with him? As if he could have made it all right. As if what those girls did — with their bigotry and stupidity — was somehow his responsibility.

All I can think is, what a waste. I mean, we have SO LITTLE TIME before he leaves for camp. I should be furious at him. But you know what? I'm not. I know he means well. And I know he cares about me, in his own weird way. So I say, "Brendan, it's not your fault."

"But I was taking you out," he replies. "I should have taken care of you. Now it's too late. The damage is done."

Damage?

AMALIA'S DILEMMA
AS SEEN BY BRENDAN

"Brendan, you are not my guardian!" I blurt out. "Look, I know how bad you feel. But I was the one who refused to come into the theater. I <u>chose</u> to stay outside, remember? The usher asked me if I wanted to go in —"

"I should have insisted —"

"And I would have said no to you

too. I didn't <u>have</u> to say yes. I'm my own person."

Brendan nods. "I — I guess I'm just . . . concerned about you. That's all."

His face is turning red. He's so uncomfortable.

Not me. I'm not uncomfortable at all now.

Just curious.

"<u>How</u> concerned?" I ask.

He stops fidgeting. I see the deep green of his eyes for the first time in a long while.

"What do you mean?" he asks back.

"You're going away. Are we supposed to miss each other?"

Brendan smiles. Something else I haven't seen in awhile. "Well . . . yeah," he says.

"So we're —?"

The bell rings. Brendan goes nowhere, and neither do I. We're just looking at each other, all alone in the hallway, and I could stay there all

day and all night. I'm thinking about
plane flights to Massachusetts and
composing letters to send beforehand,
two a day. And those green eyes are
taking me in, that beautiful green,
they're answering my question, making
me smile. And even though he was
kind of a jerk to me, I realize he
really wasn't. He was confused. So
was I. We're even.

"I guess we are," Brendan says.
"Yeah."
He takes my hand.
We fly down the hallway together
to first period.

5:21

I see Maggie in the library during
study hall. She's writing like crazy in

her spiral notebook. She doesn't even see me sit at her table.

"Hi," I say.

She practically jumps out of her seat. She smacks shut the notebook, glares at me, and grunts something that resembles a hello.

"Writing a song?" I ask.

She nods.

Then she picks up the book and calmly walks to another part of the library. A single chair with a desk attached.

I don't push it.

I see her again later, after school. I follow her outside and ask if we can talk.

"Sure. In the car."

She walks to the limo. (As usual, it's parked around the corner — not in front of the school, where other kids might see it.) Reg is holding open the door.

But instead of getting in, Maggie reaches into the bar and pulls out two bottles of liquor. Reg and I are

watching her with our jaws open as
she walks to the corner.

She dumps them both in a trash
can.

As she heads back, I see her
eyes are moist.

Silently she gets into the limo, and
I follow. Reg closes the door behind
us and races around to the driver's
seat.

"What?" Maggie asks. She's turned
away from me.

I almost forget what I was going
to say. I'm shocked at what she did,
but kind of proud too. I see she's
taking a stand, she's trying. I want to
compliment her, comfort or encourage
her — but I don't. First things first.

"I'm sorry," I tell her. "About what
I said."

She doesn't move for a long time.
Finally she just shrugs. "Why be
sorry?" she says. "You were right. I
was being harsh to my dad."

I tell her it's none of my business
how she treats her dad. She says it's

none of _her_ business whether or not I take that summer job.

I tell her the job doesn't really matter. She says I shouldn't stop living just because of her.

We're apologizing to each other, but it's weird, Nbook. It feels like we're arguing.

I realize I haven't told her what I _really_ wanted to say. "Maggie," I say to her back, "I didn't mean that comment about you wanting to be part of my family."

Up until now, Maggie's been looking out the window. Now she sits back. She looks at the floor. "I don't mean to be a pest."

I tell her she's welcome at my house any time. I admit I've been a total mess, all wrapped up in my own world. I describe my conversation with Isabel, and my dream.

She looks at me. Finally. Then she pulls a notebook out of her backpack, opens it, and holds it out.

It's a poem.

The Great Divide

I'm looking for you 'cross the wall that divides us,
A fortress of anger that totally hides us.
Alone in my world, safely apart,
The one sound I hear is the beat of my heart.
I send out a shout, but it's lost in a cloud:
I'm selfish, I'm sorry, I'm jealous and proud.
I'm lonely and hurt, I'm afraid that I blew it.
Please let me prove I'm a friend, I can do it.

© Maggie Blume

I read it. I want to say something, but I can't. No words come out, I'm so moved.

"It needs work," Maggie says. "I'm not finished yet." Like she needs to apologize. I'm a total basketcase. It's the most beautiful thing I've ever read. And I realize what an idiot I've been. I've misread Maggie just as badly as I'd misread Brendan. And Isabel.

"It's . . . great," I say. "I love it, Maggie. I love you."

That does it. We're both crying

now. Hugging each other in that backseat. I catch a glimpse of Reg's eyes in the rearview mirror, and they're smiling.

"I meant what I said, you know," Maggie finally says. "About that job. You really should take it."

"Look, if you want to protest that job, for whatever reason, I will too."

"I just want to work at the animal shelter, that's all. That's the real reason I don't want the movie job — not Dad. He isn't that awful, you know. Especially if he's not your dad."

I smile. Honestly, Nbook, I think a movie job would be <u>way</u> cool.

We sit back and put our arms around each other's shoulders. It feels great. Like old times.

After awhile, I ask Maggie about those liquor bottles she threw out.

"Mom's drinking has gotten worse," she says softly. "I'm tossing away every bottle I find that belongs to the Blume Family."

I feel like such a jerk, Nbook. Here I've been so lost in my own problems, I'm not even thinking about hers.

I tell her I'm sorry, but it sounds so feeble.

Maggie nods and looks out the window again. "Dr. Fuentes says I need to come to terms with this. She thinks I need to talk to Mom."

"Haven't you already?"

"Sort of. If I even <u>hint</u> at her drinking, she just denies anything's wrong and yells at me. Then she wobbles away and trips over the couch. I don't know if I can <u>really</u> talk to her, Amalia."

"I don't know if you can afford not to. I would, if I were you."

I cringe at my own words. I sound like Isabel.

"You don't have an eating disorder," Maggie says. "Or a dysfunctional family."

"But Maggie —"

"They both take a lot of energy. I

don't know if I have enough strength left over."

I shut my big mouth.

I can't solve her problems, Nbook. And I sure can't solve her mom's.

I can only be me. Me, who will listen and suggest and help. But mostly listen.

I guess there are some things Maggie and I will never understand about each other. And there are some answers we can never give.

But that's as it should be, isn't it?

It doesn't mean we have to stop being friends.

Sunday, 6/13

Hey, Nbook. Remember me? Sorry. I've been busy.

I'm still busy.

Just checking in before the slaughter.

Finals tomorrow.

If I flunk, don't mind the tears.

Monday, 6/14

Finals, Day 1.

Tuesday, 6/15

Only one final today. English.
Don't ask.

(Oh. Spoke to Ducky. We're set for
Friday. Dawn thinks he's picking her up
to go shopping for her trip. Instead
we'll drive to the beach.)

(Where I can contemplate another
year of eighth grade.)

Wednesday, 6/16
Home

It's over.

I'm sweating.

Maggie's convinced she aced the math and English.

It's a good thing we're friends. Otherwise I would have clocked her for saying that.

On the positive side, Isabel says all the party supplies are safe and sound at Simon's. (His pug, Schweppy, destroyed some of the plastic cutlery, but Simon bought more.) Mami and Papi don't suspect a thing.

Thursday, 6/17
After school

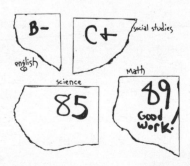

Mami thinks I'm crazy to rip up my exams. I think I'd be crazy not to. You're permanent, Nbook. And I want to remember this.

I'm a genius.

What can I tell you?

wink!

Friday, 6/18
9:01 P.M.

KIDNAPPED

A tale by Amalia Louis Stevenson

I have the best friends.

We swing by Dawn's house. We're
in our bathing suits, with stupid birthday
hats and noisemakers. We make a
huge racket. She's actually _mad_ when
she answers the door. But Ducky
wraps her in a beach towel and
says, "Take 'er aboard, mateys!" She's
screaming and laughing all the way to
the beach, and we're singing "Happy
Birthday" a hundred times at the top
of our lungs.

   Sunny has bought Dawn a bathing
suit for her birthday, so she changes
at the beach. We've prepared a
huge picnic, which Ducky has put in
the trunk — but when he opens it the
cake has fallen over and the icing is
melted. It's a total disaster but no
one cares.

   The day flies by — laughter and
swimming and volleyball and boy-
watching and all the good stuff. The
beach is swarming with other kids.

   And you'll never guess what
happens, Nbook.

   I see one of the girls.

It's not the one who spat, but it doesn't matter. I still recognize her. She's with a bunch of friends. I don't know if she recognizes me at all. Our eyes don't meet. (Frankly I don't even know if she'd remember me even if she <u>did</u> spot me.)

For a moment, part of me wants to go up to her. I don't want to spit, or punch her, or scream and yell. I have the urge to walk past her with my friends, call out "Buenos días!" in my most cheerful voice, and move on. That's all.

But the moment passes. Honestly, I'm having too good a time to think about her.

Why spoil it, Nbook?

Why ever spoil it?

Saturday, 6/19
so, so late

My head is spinning. I have been DANCING DANCING DANCING. The party is still going on. I don't think it will ever end.

Oh, Nbook, if you could just see them. Scrawny Hector has become the most handsome man in the world — and can he rhumba! Cristina is so-o-o perfect for him, so glamorous and warm and beautiful.

And guess what — she's going to have a baby! (YE≡AHH! Another cousin to play with Santos and Aurorita!) And Nelson brought his 12-string guitar and Tío Luis's voice just gets better with age, and Abuela Aurora bought me the most amazing outfit. I'm wearing the skirt, can you feel this material? And o-o-o-oh, my little cousins are so cute but destructive!

Not to mention Isabel — dear Isabel.

I love my sister.

Nbook, I solemnly promise I shall no longer mock her. (Well, at least for another week.) She arranged to get

Mami and Papi out of the house. She forced Simon Big Tooth Lover Boy to bring the party goods here on time. While I designed the decor, she did most of the grunt work. AND she remembered to invite Brendan, whom I hadn't even thought of inviting because my head has been so screwed up over these last weeks.

Anyway, all the relatives arrived here just fine — the flight, the rental car, everything was perfect — and I CAN'T BELIEVE THEY'RE HERE. I LOVE THEM SO MUCH! Am I making sense? I'm not making sense.

WHO CARES?

Sorry, Nbook, I haven't seen them in ages.

Dear Abuela, she can barely keep from crying. I know she speaks English, but she talks to me only in Spanish, telling me how proud she is of me, folding up a dollar bill in my hand — just the way she did when I was a little girl.

I try to fill her in on our move,

the town, school. My Spanish is not
great, but she listens patiently, stopping
to ask questions. At one point she
leans over to me and tells me I'm a
good girl. I've never forgotten who I
am.

I feel myself choking up. I throw
my arms around her and start to cry.
If she notices, she doesn't make a
big deal out of it. She just pats my
back and says <u>Ah, bueno</u>.

I'm crying because she's wrong. I
<u>have</u> forgotten. Big time.

I forgot who I was on that Friday
night outside the cineplex. After those
girls got ahold of me, I thought I was
nothing.

It's so easy to lose who you are,
Nbook, and so hard to get it back. I
guess you don't question your identity
until you have to. You figure, hey,
you're born with it so nothing can
affect it.

But that's not true, is it? It's more
fragile than you think. When it runs and
hides, you have to go and fetch it. You

have to let it prove how tough it really is.

Someday maybe I'll tell Abuela about what happened. She'll know what I went through. She's been through everything and she's risen above it all.

So has Tío Luis. And Papi and Mami. And just about everyone in my family, in their own ways.

I must have gotten the ability from somewhere.

That's the thing. In a way, I _am_ Abuela. I'm Mami too, and Cristina and Nelson and Aurorita and Tío Luis. I'm also my great-grandfather the farmer, my other abuela who crossed into the U.S. with nothing but a work visa and Papi in a baby blanket.

All the generations — all the dancing and music and thought and love — it's all me. Without them, I don't exist.

Does that make sense, Nbook? Because I see it so clearly. No person is alone. Everyone's part of something bigger. Something that came before. Something that has gathered strength over the years, resulting in the person you are.

Nobody can take any of that away. Ever.

So I enjoy the music. I watch my friends having a good time. I dance with Brendan and he tells me how much he loves my family.

He tells me he'll miss me too. I know I'll miss him. It's hard to believe he's leaving in three days. And that I'll start work on Maggie's dad's film in three weeks.

The summer's coming up fast.

Life will go on.

I'll go on.

But right now, it's just Vargases at the house. Everyone else has gone home. So in the meantime, maybe one more dance before bed. Maybe two.

See you.

About the Author

ANN MATTHEWS MARTIN was born on August 12, 1955. She grew up in Princeton, NJ, with her parents and her younger sister, Jane.

Although Anne used to be a teacher and then an editor of children's books, she's now a full-time writer. She gets the ideas for her books from many different places. Some are based on personal experiences. Others are based on childhood memories and feelings. Many are written about contemporary problems or events.

All of Ann's characters are made up. But some of her characters are based on real people. Sometimes Anne names her characters after people she knows; other times she chooses names she likes.

In addition to California Diaries, Ann Martin has written many other books, including the Baby-sitters Club series. She has written twelve novels for young people, including *Missing Since Monday, With You or Without You, Slam Book,* and *Just a Summer Romance.*

Ann M. Martin does not live in California, though she does visit frequently. She lives in New York with her cats, Gussie, Woody, and Willy, and her dog, Sadie. Her hobbies are reading, sewing, and needlework — especially making clothes for children.

CALIFORNIA DIARIES

Look for #15
DUCKY, DIARY THREE

Sunny and I are just friends.

I mean, I love her. But I'm not in love with her.

It doesn't matter what other people think.

Sunny and I are JUST friends.

Yeah, she's beautiful. And smart. And we laugh a lot when we're together. But we don't have that spark. Kissing her would be like kissing my sister.

Not that I have a sister. But Sunny comes closest.

So Sunny and I are JUST FRIENDS.

And we'll stay that way.

Right?